This
PJ BOOK
belongs to

_____

_____

pj Library®

JEWISH BEDTIME STORIES and SONGS

New Year at the Pier

A ROSH HASHANAH STORY

by April Halprin Wayland

illustrated by

Stéphane Jorisch

DIAL BOOKS
FOR YOUNG READERS

TASHLICH

(TAHSH-lich or tahsh-LICH; the "ch" is pronounced as in "Bach")

During Rosh Hashanah, the Jewish New Year, Jews are encouraged to reflect on their mistakes of the past year. Many Jews participate in the ceremony of Tashlich ("casting away"), one of my favorite traditions. We walk to a body of water, sing psalms, and toss pieces of stale bread into the water. Each piece of bread represents something we regret doing in the past year. Because I live near the sea, I get to toss my "mistakes" into the ocean. It can remind us to make amends. But mostly, it is a way of letting go, of creating a clean slate for the coming year. Or as Jews say, *L'shanah tovah!* "For a Good Year!" —April Halprin Wayland

AUTHOR ACKNOWLEDGMENTS: Grateful thanks to Rabbi Neil Comess-Daniels of Beth Shir Sholom Temple, Santa Monica, California, whom I interviewed a long-long-long-long time ago; Susan Dubin for years of support; Caren Stiffel, who let me read an early draft to her synagogue students; Diane Levitt, my expert in all things Jewish and a true wizard of words; Shirley Levitt for careful comments; Bruce Balan for technical support—both Talmudic and computer—and a huge dose of morals; Congregation Tikvat Jacob, Manhattan Beach, California, for the annual uplifting Tashlich celebration upon which this book is based; my agent Nancy Gallt; my editor Lauri Hornik; designer Teresa Dikun; illustrator-extraordinaire Stéphane Jorisch, whose pictures make this story soar; Jeff "gimme ferrets" Wayland, once a little boy with big hair, now a young man with big dreams; and always, always to my blue-eyed Superman, Gary.

DIAL BOOKS FOR YOUNG READERS • A division of Penguin Young Readers Group • Published by The Penguin Group • Penguin Group (USA) Inc., 375 Hudson Street, New York, NY 10014, U.S.A. • Penguin Group (Canada), 90 Eglinton Avenue East, Suite 700, Toronto, Ontario, Canada M4P 2Y3 (a division of Pearson Penguin Canada Inc.) • Penguin Books Ltd, 80 Strand, London WC2R 0RL, England • Penguin Ireland, 25 St. Stephen's Green, Dublin 2, Ireland (a division of Penguin Books Ltd) • Penguin Group (Australia), 250 Camberwell Road, Camberwell, Victoria 3124, Australia (a division of Pearson Australia Group Pty Ltd) • Penguin Books India Pvt Ltd, 11 Community Centre, Panchsheel Park, New Delhi - 110 017, India • Penguin Group (NZ), 67 Apollo Drive Rosedale, North Shore 0632, New Zealand (a division of Pearson New Zealand Ltd) • Penguin Books (South Africa) (Pty) Ltd, 24 Sturdee Avenue, Rosebank, Johannesburg 2196, South Africa • Penguin Books Ltd, Registered Offices: 80 Strand, London WC2R 0RL, England

5 7 9 10 8 6

Wayland, April Halprin.
New Year at the pier : a Rosh Hashanah story / April Halprin Wayland ; illustrated by Stéphane Jorisch.
p. cm.
Summary: On Rosh Hashanah, Izzy and his family make lists of the wrongs they have committed over the past year, and after they have apologized, they throw pieces of bread into the water to "clean their hearts" in a ceremony called Tashlich.
ISBN 978-0-8037-3279-7   [1. Tashlikh—Fiction. 2. Rosh ha-Shanah—Fiction.] I. Jorisch, Stéphane, ill. II. Title.
PZ7.W35126Ne 2009   [E]—dc22
The art was created with pen and ink, watercolor and gouache.

Special Markets ISBN: 9780803734494
CIP 082033.5K3/B0726/A6

To Bruce Balan, who knows the song in my heart
and can sing it back to me when I've forgotten the words.
—A.H.W.

To A.—S.J.

zzy loves this changing time of year. Some days sunglasses, some days sweaters. Apples, honey, the sound of the shofar, and his favorite part of Rosh Hashanah: *Tashlich*!

Everyone makes "I'm sorry" lists before Tashlich. Mom is at the patio table, writing fast. Miriam is on the grass, thinking.

Izzy puts a rock on his paper so it won't blow away. He doesn't make a list—he draws pictures. But he does count on his fingers: one, two, three. Three things he's sorry for.

What is Izzy sorry for?

He sticks up one finger. For drawing on Miriam's forehead . . . while she was asleep.

Two fingers. For losing Mom's ring . . . at the grocery store.

Three fingers. For breaking Mrs. Bickerson's drum . . . the old one they weren't even supposed to touch.

Is that it? Just three? Suddenly Izzy remembers—there's one more. Ugh. He wishes there weren't. He wishes he could forget this one.

Slowly he puts up four fingers . . . for promising he wouldn't tell anyone that Ben sucks his thumb—and then telling!

On Rosh Hashanah, as soon as they get to the synagogue, Izzy joins his friends playing tag.

"You're it!" a kid says, pointing a finger at Izzy. Izzy looks at his own finger. He runs over to his sister.

"Miriam," he whispers, "I'm sorry I drew on your forehead."

"Huh?"

"I'm sorry I drew Space Dog."

"Oh, that. No big deal," she says.

"Okay!" he says, and runs off with his friends.

When he stops to rest, Miriam looks at her list and then at Izzy. "I'm not going to call you Big Snot anymore. I'm sorry."

"I *like* being Big Snot," he says, pulling a ribbon from her hair.

"Izzy!" Miriam says, and stomps on his foot.

"Hey!" Izzy yells.

Mom walks up. "Peace, kids," she says, putting up two fingers.
Izzy looks at his own two fingers. This one is going to be harder.
"Mom?" Izzy says, looking at his shoe. "I'm sorry I lost your ring."
"I know you're sorry, sweetie—thanks. I'm sorry for something too."
His eyes get big. Mom's sorry?

"I'm sorry for always being on the phone," she says. "I'll try not to answer it when you and I are playing, okeydokey?" Mom squeezes his hand. He squeezes back.

The doors open. It's time to take their seats.

When services are over, everyone walks to the beach—Rabbi Neil,
Cantor Livia, and all the families.

At the top of the hill, Izzy counts three figures: Mrs. Bickerson
and her two dogs. Izzy looks at his three fingers. His heart
pounds like her drum used to. But maybe he doesn't have
to say it to her right now . . .

Yes. He does.

No. He doesn't.

"Well, look who's here! Hello, Izzy," says Mrs. Bickerson.

"Hi, Mrs. Bickerson," he mumbles. "Um . . . I . . ."

"Good *heavens*," Mrs. Bickerson cries
as the dogs drag her up the street.
"Sorry to be running off, dear—
come visit next week!"

Whew. Izzy runs down the hill to catch the others.

When he gets to the pier, Rabbi Neil is saying, "Tashlich is the time we apologize for things we wish we hadn't done. *Tashlich* means to throw. We throw away things we don't like or don't need. Tashlich is like cleaning your heart's closet. A new year, a clean heart."

Just this summer, Izzy and Miriam cleaned their toy closet and gave a lot away. Now it seems bigger. Sometimes he just opens the closet to see how clean it is.

They all troop up the pier singing *Avinu Malkenu*. The melody moves inside Izzy in a sad-happy way. He feels a part of the wind, a part of the waves, a part of everybody singing.

At the head of the pier, everyone crowds around Rabbi Neil and Ben's dad. They both put shofars to their lips. They blow. Whose note will last the longest?

Izzy and Miriam pretend they are blowing shofars and count to ten. They run out of breath . . . but the men keep blowing.

Izzy runs around in ten circles. He's very dizzy . . . but the men keep blowing.

Finally, Rabbi Neil's shofar runs out of sound. Ben's dad squawks out one last note. Everyone laughs and claps.

And now . . . it's time! Mom hands them slices of old bread.

Izzy rips off a piece and whispers, "This is for drawing Space Dog on Miriam's forehead." He throws it into the water.

"For Mom's ring!" Izzy says, tossing another "sorry" into the sea.

He breathes the salty air. His heart feels cleaner. And
look at those seagulls! They love Tashlich. So do the fish!

Suddenly, Ben is right next to him. "Um . . . Izzy? I'm sorry I never helped you find your yellow notebook."

His notebook? That's right—Ben *didn't* help look for it.

Just hearing Ben say he's sorry makes Izzy feel better. "That's okay," he says.

He smiles down at their four shoes side by side . . . and then remembers the fourth thing on his list. Ugh. He has to tell Ben. Well, maybe he doesn't have to . . .

Yes. He does.

They sit together on a bench looking out to sea.
Ben is bouncy and hummy. Izzy is slouchy.

Okay. Izzy takes a deep breath of ocean air.

"Ben . . . I'm sorry I told your secret."

"About sucking my thumb?"

"Yeah." The seagulls caw. "It was mean. I'm sorry."

He wishes Ben would say something.

Finally Ben says, "Izzy?"

"Yes?"

"We've been friends for a long-long-long-long time, right?"

"Right."

"So . . . because we've been friends for such a long-long-long-long time . . . you're one hundred percent forgiven."

"Really?" Izzy looks at Ben. Ben smiles.

"Okay—and from now on, I promise to keep your secrets *secret*!" Izzy says, feeding a piece of bread to Ben.

"And I promise to help you look for everything you lose," Ben says.

They toss pieces of bread out to the fish. Izzy's heart feels as big as the ocean. But what about Mrs. Bickerson?

Izzy decides he will talk to her. Soon. He throws another piece into the sea. "For Mrs. Bickerson's drum!"

Ben and Izzy toss the last bits into the wind.

Izzy loves this changing time of year. Some days sunglasses, some days sweaters. The sound of the shofar and the salty smell of the sea. Time to think about his family and this whole wide, windy world.

Everyone sings one last song. Then they slowly walk home, holding hands in a family-and-friends chain, with empty bread bags . . .

. . . and clean, wide-open hearts.